The Christmas Carol

From the story
by
CHARLES DICKENS

Scrooge was a mean, old miser who didn't care for anyone or anything...except his money.

He disliked everything. Most of all, he hated Christmas. When someone would wish him a "Merry Christmas," he would grumble, "Bah, humbug!"

Poor Bob Cratchit was working late for Scrooge again. He very much wanted to go home to his family. After all, it was Christmas Eve.

Finally, old Scrooge allowed Cratchit to leave. "Would you like to spend Christmas with my family?" he asked Scrooge.

"Nonsense! Christmas, bah humbug! Now leave me alone. I have work to do!" Scrooge answered.

Late that night, Mr. Scrooge went home to his dark house. As he got to his door, the knocker appeared to turn into the face of his partner, Jacob Marley, who had died years ago.

Frightened, Scrooge hurried inside and went straight to his bedroom. He changed into his nightshirt and crawled into bed.

"Ebenezer Scrooo-ooge!" a voice cried out in the dark room. Suddenly a ghost appeared, covered in locks and chains!

"Marley, why do you haunt me?" said Scrooge, shaking with fright.

"To save you from yourself, Ebenezer!" the ghost cried. "Tonight you will be visited by three spirits who will show you the *true* meaning of Christmas!"

"Ghosts and spirits indeed!" growled Scrooge as he drifted off to sleep. As the clock struck one o'clock, the first of three spirits appeared.

"Ebenezer Scrooo-ooge," a voice called. "I am the Ghost of Christmas Past, said the spirit. "Come with me."

"Where are we?" asked Scrooge.

"Have you forgotten your childhood, Ebenezer?" asked the spirit.

"Why this is my old schoolhouse," Scrooge said with surprise.

"Yes, Ebenezer. That little child sitting alone is you."

"Many a Christmas you spent alone without friends or family," said the spirit. "Money became your only joy and love."

Scrooge saw himself as a young man again. Beside him was a women, Belle. "I had almost forgotten how beautiful she was," Scrooge sighed.

"You were to marry her, remember?" asked the spirit. "But gold was more important to you."

"No! Spirit, take me away. Forgive me, Belle!" cried Scrooge.

When Scrooge looked up, he was back in his room and the spirit was gone.

"Ebenezer Scrooo-ooge!" called a voice.

"Come closer," the spirit roared. "I am the Ghost of Christmas Present. Come with me, you have a great deal to learn tonight."

"Who's little house is this?" asked Scrooge. "This is the house of your clerk, Bob Cratchit," answered the spirit.

The spirit pointed to the door. In the doorway was Bob, with his son, Tiny Tim, high upon his shoulder.

"Merry Christmas!" Bob called to his family as he hugged his wife.

"And how's our Tiny Tim?" asked Bob. "I believe he's getting stronger every day."

"Of course he is," Mrs. Cratchit said, holding back a tear as Tiny Tim hobbled to his stool.

"I didn't know the child was sick," said Scrooge.

"Would you have cared, Ebenezer?" asked the spirit.

"Spirit," said Scrooge. "Tell me, will Tiny Tim live?"

"I see an empty stool and a crutch in the corner. If these shadows remain unchanged, the child will die."

"No, spirit," Scrooge begged. "Don't let the boy die!"

"It is not by my kindness that he will live, but by yours, Ebenezer...if you *truly* care. Come now!" said the spirit.

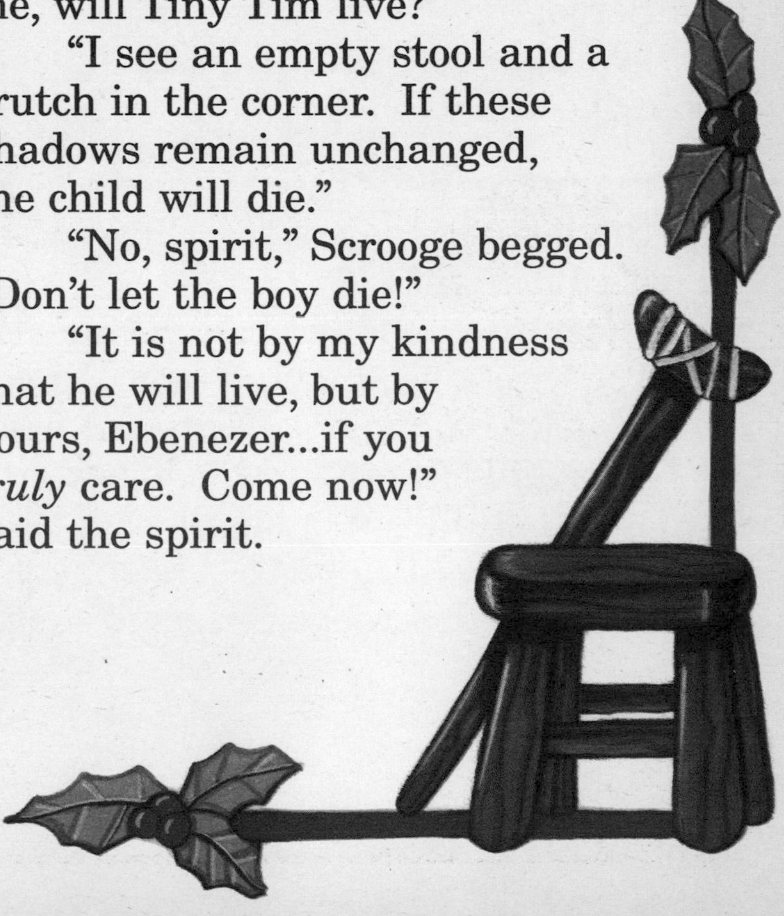

Scrooge traveled with the spirit to see many families, both rich and poor, to see the love and joy of the Christmas spirit that night.

"Before you leave, tell me spirit, what is that I see moving beneath your robe?" asked Scrooge. The Spirit opened his robe and clinging to his legs were two small children: a small, ragged boy and a forlorn, little girl. "Are they yours Spirit?" asked Scrooge.

"This boy is *Ignorance*. This girl is *Want*. Beware them both," the spirit said sadly, then disappeared.

Scrooge stood shivering in the new-fallen snow. He turned to find himself before a dark and gloomy spirit.

"Are you the Ghost of Christmas Yet to Come?" asked Scrooge. The spirit said nothing, but nodded in reply.

The spirit fixed his eyes upon Scrooge, then pointed a bony finger toward the mist.

"Lead on, spirit," moaned Scrooge.

The spirit said nothing. Scrooge then saw what he dreaded most...the empty stool and the little crutch of Tiny Tim.

"No, spirit no!"
Scrooge cried out.
"Tell me it isn't so."

Scrooge began to weep. As he raised his head, he found he was in a graveyard. The spirit was pointing to a tombstone.

Scrooge drew close to the grave. There on the headstone was his name, EBENEZER SCROOGE.

"No, spirit! I will be a better man! Please! No, no!" Scrooge suddenly awoke on Christmas morning to find himself back in his own bed. The spirits had done their work in one night!

Excitedly, Scrooge ran to the window and threw open the shutters.

"Merry Christmas!" shouted Scrooge. Then, as he spotted a passing boy, he called out, "Boy! Hurry! Go down the street and buy the big turkey that hangs in the butcher's shop and take it to Bob Cratchit's house!" He tossed a large bag of gold coins down to the boy.

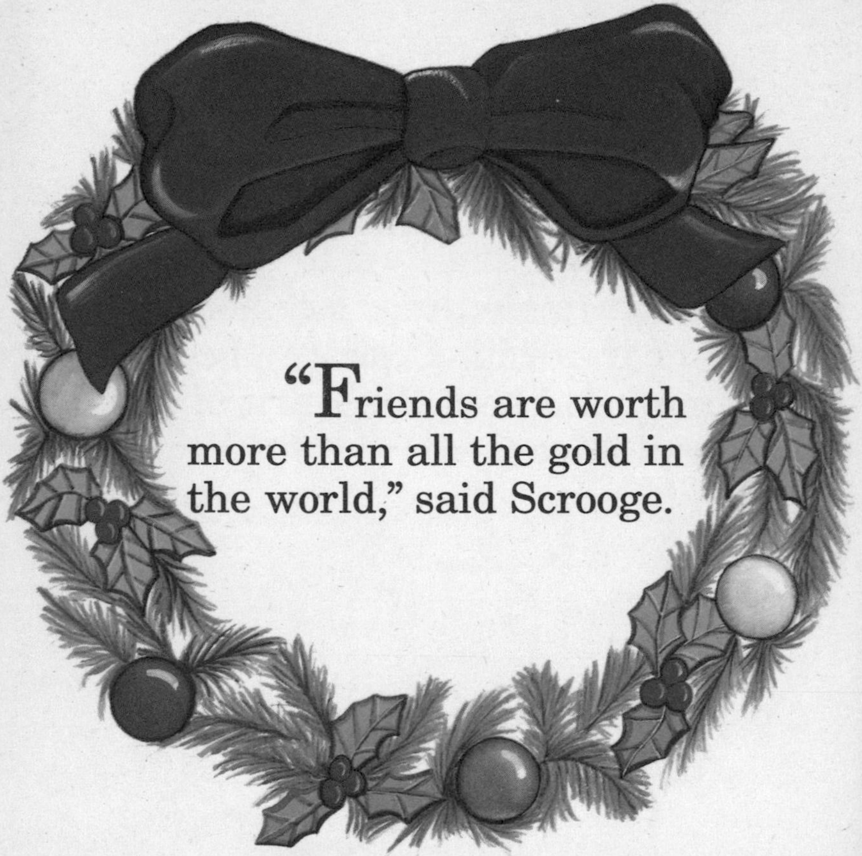

"Friends are worth more than all the gold in the world," said Scrooge.

From then on, he made sure Bob Cratchit and his family had all the good food and warm clothing they needed.

After that night, Scrooge became a better man and kept the spirit of Christmas alive.